I0537460

PHOBIA

BY: KP GREEN

Who am I? I am asking myself this question as I look in the mirror at my reflection. I don't recognize this person. Somewhere along the line I lost myself but, as I think about it more, I never really knew the real me. So, I just stare and, in my mind I am taking a picture and remembering every feature: my manageable hair that I possibly inherited from my mother's side of the family that is now down my back, my low, tight eyes, the dark circles around my eyes that I've had since I can remember...

I am memorizing every mole, every scar, my fairly large nose, my plump lips and round face. I don't find myself beautiful even though I have been told this before. But, I think they say that I am trying to make me feel

good about myself. I drop my head as a tear escapes my eyes. And when I look back up, I am staring at a fraction of myself. The child in me that is yearning for that true love, that self love that I manage to portray daily to my peers but don't really have. I am lost and alone. And, no one knows because I put on this mask and walk around as if I have it all together when in reality I don't.

I take a deep breath and close my eyes because I know when I walk back out into this world, I will have to smile and act like I have my life together. I have to act like I don't care what people think of me. I have to act like I have this confidence that is beyond anything or anyone that I've ever known. So, I straighten my shoulders, give myself one last look

and put on my million dollar smile. If only everyone knew who I really am. How could they when I don't even know? I've searched for myself in other women and I've longed for love from the wrong men. I have to find myself. But, where do I start?

My name is LaKimma Reed but everyone calls me Kimme. Although people make mistakes in life I feel that this one is a bit much. Nevertheless, it did not stop me from doing the same dreadful thing again. Before I tell you my secret, let me tell you a story of a lonely girl seeking the love from every man she's come in contact with that she feels she didn't receive from her father. Here's her story! Are you ready?

"Either, write something worth reading or do something worth writing"

~Benjamin Franklin~

CHAPTER 1

"Who is this and who are you here for?" My mom asks the person who is banging on her front door at a quarter to midnight. She had just made it home from pulling a double shift at the warehouse that she works at seven days a week to support my two older twin sisters and I. I know who it is and who the person is looking for but I deny, deny, deny! Until, the person at the door says, "I'm here for Kimma". What did he say that for? It is a dude who is almost twice my age at the door asking for me. I am only ten years young but, I have been telling this dude that I am sixteen. I have a very mature voice for my age. So, I could go for much older over the phone. If looks

could kill, I'd be dead on sight with the look my mom gave me when he mentioned my name but, of course I'm still sticking to deny, deny, deny. So I say, "He must be talking about another Kimma because it's not me". My mom gives me this "like really" face. How many people really have that name?

After a pause from my mom, he goes on. "She told me to come over here and meet her and her sisters at this address but I don't know her sister's names." My sisters had long ago abandoned me, one locked up in the bathroom and the other playing possum (asleep). So, I am stuck to defend myself when they were the ones who wanted the company and used me. I was a sucker to play along. Who knew that our

mom would get off early?! "Well, if you don't leave my house right now, I am calling the police" Mom says. By this time, she's beet red because she is fair skinned and I am in my room now shaking in my skin because I know once dude and his crew leaves, all hell is going to break loose.

My mom's name is Shanice. I have been giving her such a hard time and I don't try to but I am just a little rebellious child that wants some love and attention. She does that best that she can with us and I don't make it any better.

I hear them walk down the apartment complex stairs and I glance out the windows. Keep in mind that we've never met. We have only conversed on the phone

and I just wanted to see his face. BAD MISTAKE! He spots me peeking out of the blinds and shouts, "Yo, Kimma! Come on out!" My mom burst into the room and beats me like I stole something. Afterwards, she calls my Dad, Kharo, who only acts like one when I get into trouble, to hear him try to reprimand me but, I am only half listening because I don't want to hear that mess. My mom and Dad split up about three years ago after our paternal grandmother died. My grandmother was the one that held the family together, you know. When she passed, everyone who was living under her roof, left. My dad put my mom through so much crap that I guess she got fed up.

I must have drifted off or something because I could hear my dad shouting through the phone. "Kimma, Kimma! Do you hear me?' "Yeah I hear you" I said. "What did I say then?" he shouts. "Blah, blah, blah" I said. "Don't make me come to Mississippi and whoop your ass." And, in my mind I'm saying, "Please do!" "These boys only want one thing from you and you're too young to even be thinking about what they want" he said. I hadn't seen my father since he and mom split up and I missed him terribly. I'd never let him or anyone know that because I didn't want to appear weak. A ten year old girl wanting her father is weak, right? Maybe. But, he should've been there. He makes all of these promises like he always does about coming to see us. I

know he isn't because he is too busy trying to find himself. He doesn't have time for his children who need him.

Meanwhile, my mom is in her room crying a river for what I've just done and I start to feel a little bad. My sisters finally make their way out of the bathroom and fake sleeping after I get off the phone with dad and they figure the coast is clear. I am sitting on the bed with my arms crossed waiting on an explanation from the both of them for sticking me under the gun like that. Shanna, my oldest sister, spoke first. "I thought she was gone kill you! Momma wasn't about to tear me a new a-hole because of this mess. Besides, you would've done the same thing to us. We just beat you to it." I heard my second oldest sister, Quanna, chuckle.

"What are you laughing at, rat?" I asked her. You played sleep the entire time. "Let me tell you something. I don't want no dealings with you and Shanna's shenanigans. I played sleep to keep from getting interrogated by momma. Y'all know she asks a lot of questions and I didn't want to be caught up in it." Shanna said, "You were the one that invited them, Quanna." " I'm the one who got tore out the frame for y'all" I shouted. *Shhh* the twins said before you start momma up again. Just then ma shouted, "Y'all better take y'all ass to bed before I come in there." We knew to do as she said because even though ma was a crier, when she cried she was brutal and would wipe you out like Hurricane Katrina. We all went to bed that night not knowing

what momma's attitude would be like the next day.

A week later, our mom hit us with the news that we would be moving in with our dad. We cried and begged her to let us stay with her but she wouldn't bulge. We moved in with him and his at the moment girlfriend, Maxine. I hated every minute of it and the fact that she chose me to pick on didn't make it any better. One day while our dad was at work, she locked me in a room for nine hours. My sister received the whooping of a lifetime not to open their mouths about it or she'd tell our dad that we stole some money that came up missing out of his wallet that was for rent and utilities. He had to work double shifts to get it back which left us with her more. When

going on. This continued for a couple of years and now, she was "pleasuring" me as well. My sisters got beatings repeatedly and I was molested repeatedly. Our dad never noticed the change in our behavior and we never told him. He was too busy making sure she was happy to notice. He never saw the signs.

One day though, out of the blue, our mom called and said that she was ready for us to come home and our dad was all too ready to oblige because his girlfriend had started complaining about starting a family and we were in the way. My sisters and I were so happy to get out of that hell hole that we didn't care about what we had gone through the last two years. But, that night when we made it home to our mom, we

made a vow to never mention what had happened while staying with our dad ever again. We cried and held each other and never told a soul.

CHAPTER 2

Six months later….

"Hey, boy! My sister likes you and she wants your number." My friends and I found this random guy at our school and started to pick with Shanna about him. "I don't like that little-headed boy." Shanna said and we all burst into fits of laughter. I am twelve now and my sisters are thirteen. We're at a new school and I clicked with some of the other kids immediately. The twins had friends as well but, they ran in different circles from me and my friends. We were on our way to P.E. class and we saw the cutie and just decided to have

some fun. Quanna had a different schedule altogether so she was in Math class.

We make it to the gym and start our exercise routine. All of a sudden, the same cutie I was teasing my sister about walks up to me and slides a piece of paper in my pocket. At first, I thought he was trying to cop a feel but it happened so fast that I didn't have time to react. When P.E. was over and I went to study hall, I pulled the paper out and realized that it was his name and number. His name was Mercy. I showed my friend, Neka, who happens to have every class with me. Her being the crazy friend that she is, shouted, "You go, girl!" I started crying laughing because she was

trying to do the dougie but couldn't dance. This got us kicked out of class.

Later that Friday night, I tried calling Mercy and he was gone to the football game. Our mom never let us do anything like that because she was afraid we would meet a guy or some craziness. We couldn't even converse with boys on the phone because she said that it would lead to other things like; kissing and having sex which, she probably was right. Hell, I was ready to experience sex and didn't even know what it was yet.

A week went by before I finally got him on the phone. I know that we go to school together but, I had to catch up on school work. Even though I was ready for love, I

didn't know what love was and I had never had a boy interested in me before. Even though outside I had it all together, I was a nervous wreck just talking to him over the phone.

Once I got school work out of the way, my time was spent getting to know Mercy. We found ways to sneak out of class, sneak kisses here and there, and get a little feel from time to time. We did this so often that we started getting caught by the school principal who now knew us on a first name basis. I used to go to bed early just to wake up before midnight to sneak on the phone and talk to him for hours. My mom even caught us once and I was so embarrassed. Mercy made fun of me that next day and I pushed him into a brick wall. We were so in

love or so I thought. We were almost two years drama free and then this new girl came to the school and screwed everything up.

"Kimma, Kimma! My friends shout while running up to me. Girl! You should have been at Roller World Saturday. We saw Mercy grinding all up on Sierra during social." "Who, the new girl?" I asked. "Yeah, her" all of my friends say in unison. I knew that I was going to have a bad day with them coming to me with this as soon as we got off the bus. Now, I'm searching for him waiting for his bus which I find hasn't made it to the school yet. He tries to avoid me all day but I catch up with him during lunch. "Mercy! I heard that you were dancing and grinding up on Sierra at Roller World this

weekend. Is this true?" By this time a small crowd has formed around us and I am furious. "Not now, Kimma! I don't want to talk about this right now" Mercy says and walks off. My friends are looking at me sideways like I'm not supposed to take that. I just dart to the restroom and cry my eyes out for the rest of the day skipping my last two classes.

In between classes my friends check on me and bring me new information each time. Sierra lives in the same projects where he lives and is giving him her "goods" and this makes her easy for him. I am so insecure at this point and feel so inadequate that I draw up in a ball on the floor of the restroom and finish crying my eyes out until the bell rings to go home. I make it home

and go straight to bed to make sure I meet

our phone call date for that night.

CHAPTER 3

RING, RING

 Mercy answers. "Hello! I've been waiting on your call all night. I wanted to talk to you today about what happened at the skating rink Saturday." By this time, I am crying again but I manage to speak. "I want to believe that you didn't do what they said and right now I'm willing to let it go if you tell me that you didn't do it." I'm hopeful after all because I love the kid, you know. He takes a deep breath and says, "I did dance with her but, it meant nothing." My heart drops into the pit of my stomach, y'all. He crushed me with just that but, I take it further. "Did you have sex with her too?" I hold my breath. He takes another

deep breath and tells me that he did in fact sleep with her but, that too, meant nothing to him. At that moment, it felt like the wind had been knocked out of me.

"Maybe we should take a break for a while because I can't handle this" I tell him. "No, Kimma! Mane! Damn, mane! Shit! I messed up but I promise that I'll never do it again. It's just that you're a virgin and I have needs. I don't want to pressure you because I love you." I shout, "YOU LOVE ME! No! You love the pussy. Otherwise, you wouldn't have cheated on me. We need to take a break." I slam the phone down waking up Shanna but Quanna is still snoring. "What you doing on the phone? Ma is going to wake up and catch you again, Kimma. Why are you crying?" she says as

she notices my tears. "I found out that Mercy has been cheating on me." I burst out as new tears fell from my eyes. "Well, that's what you get! First, you try to hook him up with me. Then, you end up with him. You wanted him from the start didn't you?" she blurts out. Now, I'm looking at her like she has grown a second head. "Are you serious right now? I was playing with you and you said that you didn't like him. I found out that he liked me and I went for it. If I would've known that you actually liked him, I never would've started dating him, Shanna. I'm not like that" I whisper scream. "Whatever! You deserve whatever he throws at you" she says. And, she turns over and goes back to bed leaving me shocked and hurt by her words.

2 weeks later...

I still hadn't forgiven Mercy but, it still didn't stop him from trying to get me back. One day, he pulled me to the side as we were changing classes and he looked so sad. "Kimma, please call me tonight, same time. Please!" He walked off and didn't look back. I thought it was strange but I didn't let it bother me because I was still upset with him. I still loved him but I was still hurting.

When I got home from school I decided to call him. Our mom was working a better job. So, we had a little more freedom. Shanna and I were still not speaking to each other. And, Quanna was still in her own little world.

I call him and he immediately informs me that he is about to move to California to live with his mom and he'd stay if I gave him another chance. I was speechless because I never expected him to leave me even though we were having problems. I still couldn't bring myself to forgive and forget yet though. So, I played hard to get and told him to let me think about it. I called him the next day to tell him that I'd give him another chance only to find out that he had decided to leave anyway. He would be leaving at the end of the school year and staying in California for a year. At that moment, even though we weren't really together, I decided to lose my virginity to him. He was my first love. So, it felt right to lose it to him. We met up at my cousin's

house. She was older than us but she was cool and let us do pretty much whatever we wanted.

Our first attempt was a failure but I was determined to do it because he would be leaving soon. Our second attempt, we succeeded. After we were done, I noticed a lot of blood and began to panic. He calmed me down though and explained that he "popped my cherry" which is normal for some virgins. I still felt lost. I don't know why but, I thought that after I gave myself to him that I would feel whole. For some reason I just felt violated and he noticed because I was unconsciously hugging myself as we waited outside for his ride to come pick him up. He came over and wrapped his arms around me and asked, "Why are you

standing there like I just raped you or something?" I was in a daze and didn't answer. He put his finger under my chin and raised my head so that I could look into his eyes. "Kimma, promise me that you'll wait for me while I'm in California. I know that we aren't together but, I love you....wait for me!" "If you loved me, you wouldn't be leaving me" I state. "What's done is done now. Just please, wait for me. We can fix this when I get back to Mississippi." I just looked at him and said that I would. Why? I don't know. The fact was I loved him and would do anything for him.

CHAPTER 4

1 year later....

"Kimma, I thought that you were going to wait for me?" Mercy is back from California and while he was gone, I met someone. Don't jump to conclusions though because while he was in California, he slept with a few females which just had me fed up with his ass. "You should have thought about that before you started putting your thing in all those girls up there. What I look like waiting on someone who I am not even with when he can't even wait for me in return?" I was so mad that my breathing was irregular and I was sure that my blood pressure was up. "We weren't together. So,

I figured I could have a little fun while I was there. After all, I am still a man!" This dude has lost his mind for real. "Well, why ask me to wait for you if you didn't plan on doing the same? This new boy is nothing like you, Mercy. I don't have to worry about him cheating on me and I am not leaving him for you." We were in between classes and I didn't have time for his foolishness. I was a ninth grader now and he, an eleventh grader. I was over him.

Time went on and Mercy had gotten tired of hounding me to give him another chance. He even stated one day that a guy could only wait so long before he gave up. Good! I didn't want him anyway. I had the dude that I wanted.

His name is Cane. I met him through our cousins that were dating at the time. My cousin, Nia was dating his cousin, Mike and they hooked us up. Mercy never gave up though. He was persistent. I ignored him because I was in love with Cane now. Cane was the first boy that my mom let come over and call the house and I was on cloud nine. It was short lived because not even a year into our relationship, I became pregnant. I was not prepared for the whirlwind that my life was about to take.

It shouldn't come as a shock to you that I have horrible timing. Right before I found out I was pregnant, Cane and I had this big fight about some he say she say mess and we were beefing big time. So me being the unstable person that I am was ready to get

back with Mercy. On top of me being pregnant, my dad and mom were trying to mend their relationship at the same time. My mom whooped me when she found out with a belt like I was some little kid. I know you guys are wondering how my mom found out I was pregnant. SHANNA! She was determined to ruin my life. She blurted it out one day while she and I were having an argument. Quanna, always quiet and calm, just watched everything unfold. My mom went right on to the nearest store and bought a pregnancy test. Low and behold, here we are. Shanna has been a hater ever since she "claims" I stole Mercy from her. I'm telling y'all, this chick is delusional or something.

I tried to rekindle a relationship with Mercy because I am angry with Cane. Shanna finds out about what I am doing and spreads my pregnancy throughout the entire school. Mercy finds out and cuts all contact with me. He walks past me at school like he doesn't see me and, other times he just dodges me all together. I'm starting to regret not giving him another chance because I realize after I get pregnant by Cane, that I still have feelings for Mercy.

Eventually, I come to reality though and start to focus on my relationship with Cane because we are about to be parents. Everything was going good too! I started showing after a while and everyone knew about the pregnancy. He was allowed to come over more and sleep over sometimes

because my mom said that the damage had already been done. Of course my dad was out of our lives again. My sisters and I were used to it because he had been in and out of lives for as long as we could remember.

We found out that I was having a boy and Cane was super excited as any man would be. We both were scared because we were so young and we knew nothing about raising a baby. After that everything went pretty fast.

I went into labor in the middle of the night. I was awakened out of my sleep with cramps but really didn't pay them any mind. When I finally got up and went to the restroom, I realized that I was bleeding. I screamed and woke everybody up. My

mom rushed me to the hospital only to be sent home because I wasn't dilated enough. I did a lot of walking to bring my baby down and by 5 o'clock that same morning, I was in labor.

I had complications while trying to birth my son. His heartbeat stopped when they burst my sack and everyone started to panic. I looked to my left and my mom, sisters, cousin, and Cane's sister, Shelly, we all were in tears. I didn't know how bad it was at the time because I was in and out of consciousness due to the meds the nurse had given me. I remember hearing a faint heartbeat and being rushed to have an emergency cesarean. I didn't have time to

digest what was happening because I was out again due to the anesthetics.

I came to with a start and asked, "Where is my son?" "He's fine and well. He is resting in the nursery" the nurse said. I breathed a sigh of relief and asked when I could see him. The nurse informed me that as soon as I am done in observation, they would bring him to my room. When I see my son's face, everything that I've gone through was worth it. I had Cane, my son was healthy and my mom was finally over the pregnancy. Life was good!

CHAPTER 5

"Miss Reed, you have Chlamydia!" the little old nurse at my local health department states. "WHAT!" I shout and actually scare the poor lady. "That's impossible, Miss. I've only had one partner for the past two years. There is no way I have Chlamydia." "Well honey, you may need to have a talk with that partner because you definitely have the disease. Have you ever had a disease before?" the nurse asks. "No ma'am" I half snort out due to me crying hysterically. Her face softens and she places her hand over mine on her desk. "Sweetie, these things happen sometimes. You just have to be more careful because once you catch your first

disease; it's like opening up a can of worms!" The nurse did her best to console me but I just couldn't calm down. She left me alone to compose myself and when she returned with my antibiotics, I had somewhat returned to my normal self. I had to get myself together before I stepped out of that room in front of all the other people waiting to hear their fate. I left the clinic in a daze because I knew that I had been faithful to Cane. Before today, I thought that he had been as well. So now, I am sixteen with a baby and an STD. Thank God that it was at least curable.

I go to Cane's house where he lives with his mom and explain to him the news that I had just received and this fool tells me that I must've cheated on him and caught the

STD from some other guy because I didn't catch it from him. I was devastated because in my mind, if he doesn't have anything, how did I get it?! Crazy, I know. Keep in mind that he is the second guy that I've slept with and I didn't really know much about diseases and how they are transmitted. So, I basically let it go. I mean, what else was there for me to do? A few months went by before I learned the truth.

Cane and his cousin, May, were talking one day and I overheard their conversation. They thought that I was still asleep on the couch. They were whispering and Cane explained that he was the one that had given me the STD. He got it from one of his ex-girlfriends that he was still sleeping with. When I heard this, I became shocked, hurt,

and very angry. Our son, who was now three months, was there sleeping beside me. I got up and went in the kitchen where they were and when I walked in, they both paused. I stood there with my arms crossed and my foot tapping the floor. "How could you do that to me?" I asked Cane. "What you mean?" He asked trying to play dumb. "I heard everything that you said, Cane. How could you have me think that I somehow contracted a disease that I know nothing about from another guy that does not exist knowing that you gave it to me the entire time? I would've never done you like that. Why? Why mess up my life and hurt me after you know what I've been through?" I was now trembling and crying uncontrollably. I began to fall to the floor

but before I could hit it, Cane caught me and tried his best to soothe me. I will never forget that this dude that I love so deeply could hurt me so bad. I felt so betrayed and used. We broke up after that and I was just numb to all of the nonsense.

CHAPTER 6

"Girl, you got a tongue ring now?" Cane's mom asked me one day when I was dropping our kids off at her house. It has been another couple of years and Cane and I managed to have another child in the midst of our breaking up and getting back together. We had our son, Kel, who was now two years old and our daughter, Kim, who was only five months. We were on one of our "off" seasons again so; we were both doing our own thing. Cane was in the streets as usual and didn't have a job and neither did I. We were both still living at home with our parents and I was just using what I had to get what I wanted. Before you judge me, know that I'll do anything to take

care of my kids. I had a lot of different clients and they paid top dollar for the pussy and this fire head. I was always safe and wrapped it up because I couldn't take any chances getting another STD.

"Yes! I got my tongue pierced but, it's just for decoration" I lied. She gave me that look that your grandma gives when she knows that you're telling a fib. "Well, just be careful out there. Be safe because you know that you have to be here for these kids." Man! Old people be knowing what's up. I almost tear up but manage a "Yes, ma'am". She begins to walk back into the house but, not before telling me to bring my kids some diapers and wipes.

I am potty training my son but they keep him in diapers which defeat the purpose. I drive off thinking about what my mother in law said and I come to the conclusion that I am tired of using my body for money. Cane does what he can for his kids when he can. It's just sometimes that's not enough.

He also has my kids around his lady friends and that's something that I do not approve of and I find it so disrespectful because I make sure my kids are gone or asleep before I handle my "business". How do I know he has my kids around these different females? My two year old brags about how they all take him to the store and buy him and his sister candy, chips and toys. Now, I wouldn't mind it if he was married and had

my kids around his wife. It's a big problem though with these random chicks.

In the midst of all of this, Mercy is back in my life. I know that this is the same boy that hurt little, innocent Kimma. Now, I'm far from little and I'm five years past innocent. I'll give it to him though, he was my first love and I'm still in love with him. This is the only reason why he gets the pussy for free along with Cane.

Mercy asked to start back kicking with me again and I let him. He's angry with me though because he feels that he's been kicking it with me longer than Cane but Cane and I have kids together. He'll get over it! I know that I sound like a bitter bitch. I AM! I have lost all respect for everyone,

even me. I'm all about getting my paper now because it will always keep me happy.

Mercy lives somewhere up north now; I never cared to ask where. I just care about him giving me the dick when he's in town. He even went as far as saying that we would never be more than friends with benefits and that's cool with me because I've got bigger stuff to worry about.

One night we were chilling on a back road after giving him one of my specials and he just blurted out, "What happened to you, Kimma? You used to have a little more finesse about yourself. Now, you're just a hoe!" I stayed calm. However, my voice was a deadly whisper. "First of all, what I do is my fucking business. Second of all, if I am

such a hoe, why do you keep coming back? Third of all, you contributed to the person that I am today. So, you can keep that shit to yourself. Only thing you care about anyway is getting your dick wet. So, stop acting like you have a heart all of a sudden." He was speechless and he should be. He had a good thing then fucked it up, so I was good. "As a matter of fact, let me take you back to your grandma's house because I am done right now." I started the car and sped off.

I didn't need him or anybody else judging me because no one was perfect. People tend to hide what they do behind closed doors. But me, I don't care what people see or say about me because I take care of me and mine. I was fed up with men and with

life. My life has been disappointment after disappointment; heartache after heartache and, I was tired. When I made it home from dropping Mercy off, I did what any other person who is tired of life does, I tried taking mine.

I was home alone. Our mom was out of town again, something she did quite often now. I have no idea where my sisters were. I went to my mom's medicine cabinet and took her bottle of prescription painkiller out. I went to the kitchen and got my mom's wine that she drinks when the mood hits her and just started downing the pills handfuls at a time with the alcohol. After about ten minutes of doing this, I started to feel woozy and droopy. The wine bottle and pills slipped from my hand and before I

knew it everything went black. I was finally at peace. It felt like I was dreaming and the only thing that kept replaying in my mind were my kids and I began to weep inside for them. All of a sudden, it felt like a strong pull and my eyes opened to bright lights. When my eyes finally adjusted, I realized that I was in a hospital and when I looked around, the first face I saw was Cane's.

"What..." I try to speak but my throat is as dry as the Sahara desert. Immediately he gets the cup of melting ice cubes off of the bedside table. I drink and the water instantly soothes my burning throat. "What happened? Where are the kids, my mom, and sisters?" He gives me this look of something that I can't quite describe. I think that I saw love in his eyes but, I know that

he doesn't love me. He cares for me because after all, I am the mother of his only two children. "You tried to take your life last night. Kimma! Baby, what were you thinking? You know that the kids and I need you" he says. The night before came flashing back to me. The wine, the pills, and the pain that I felt after Mercy told me how much of a whore I was, came rushing back to me. I tried to sit up and get out of bed. "Calm down, baby. The doctor said that you had to take it easy for a while." Just before I could tell him a piece of my mind, a nurse walked in.

"How are you Miss Reed? You gave us quite a scare. The nurse checks my vitals

and asks if I am in any pain. "I feel a little tired but otherwise, I'm okay" I say. "Good!

The doctor will be in with you shortly." The nurse gives me a reassuring smile and walks out of the room. And like clockwork, in walks the doctor. "Hi. Miss Reed. I am Dr. Jacobs. You almost overdosed on pain medication and your mom says that you've been having migraines a lot lately. She states that this could be the reason you took so many pills in one day. Can you tell me what happened?" I couldn't believe it! My mom had actually covered for me or she probably did think that was the case. "Well. I've been having these really bad migraines and they wouldn't go away no matter what I'd take. I then remembered that my mom had these prescription painkillers. So, I just

started taking them and taking them because I wanted the pain to go away. I didn't mean to take so many. That's all that I remember." I was hoping and praying that he bought my story because I was fully aware that my kids could be taken away from me for what I'd done. "Miss Reed, you took a lot of pain killers and with alcohol. Do you understand how dangerous that is? You're blessed because situations like this usually do not end well." I looked over at Cane and he was just staring at me. "I know and I made a mistake. It will never happen again." I was crying now. Dr. Jacobs added, "We will keep you a couple more days to run some test to make sure everything is okay and then, you're free to go." "Yes sir.

And, thank you!" He simply nods and walks out of the room.

"Kimma, I love you and what happened to you has helped me realize that I still want to be with you so we can both be here for our kids. And just like that, we were on again! I was vulnerable and he wanted me. Even if it was only for a moment, I would cherish it.

CHAPTER 7

1 year later....

Cane and I have our own place now. It may be in the heart of the ghetto and infested with spiders and roaches but, it's ours. I got a job working at the local supermarket and Cane still wasn't working; because of that everything was on me. He may as well have been working though because he left the house at the crack of dawn and came home late every night. Most of the time, I had to find a ride to and from work because he was always in the car. Since we've been back together things have been interesting to say the least.

We've dabbled in things that have spiced up our sex life such as; threesomes, adult toys and everything else imaginable. Our sex life has been fun which is why I don't understand his sudden distance from me.

It really shouldn't have come as a shock to me when I found out that I was pregnant, AGAIN! That would make me 19 years old with three kids and the timing couldn't have been any worse. I was barely able to support the two kids that I already have. When Cane made it home that evening, I showed him the pregnancy test and he was speechless; while he couldn't talk, I couldn't stop crying. I finally calmed down and we decided that we just couldn't afford any more kids right now. It would just be too much on us. So, we made the decision to

terminate the pregnancy. It was the hardest one that we had to make and I was devastated.

"Kimma, wake up!" Case said while nudging me. "Dang, C. I didn't even know I had fallen asleep." I yawned and stretched. "Are you sure that you're okay because you've been extremely quiet and staring off into space and it's scaring me?" she says glancing at me and trying to watch the road as she drives. "I just feel like I've made a big mistake by aborting my child, Case. I know that we can't afford another child but, I feel like there was another way. Do you think that I made a mistake?" I asked her. "Look! I'm not here to judge you. That's something that you had to decide on. Just don't ask me to bring you up here again because I'm

not doing it, cuz." I understood her though and I couldn't blame her. I wouldn't have known about this clinic that does one day services had it not been for her though. I just couldn't shake the funk that I was in and I was starting to become depressed in the last two hours it had taken us to make it back to Mississippi.

For the rest of the ride home we remained silent. I guess Case knew that I just needed some time and she gave me that. I was thinking about whether my baby would've been a boy or girl. Who would she/he resemble? So many things were going through my mind that I couldn't even keep up. Cane didn't want to go with me even though the decision was mutual that I get an abortion. I think that was for the best.

We finally made it back to my house and I was relieved. I just wanted to shower and lie down because I was not in the mood for anything else. Before sending Case on her way, we agreed not to ever speak of this again.

 I made it to what I assumed was an empty house because my kids are at my mom's and Cane is never home this early in the evening. I make my way into our tiny apartment and it doesn't take me long to hear noises coming from our bedroom. I dropped everything, careful to be quiet, and put my ear up to the door to make sure my ears weren't playing tricks on me. I was pretty sure that the noise I was hearing was definitely from someone getting down and dirty. I jiggle the door handle and realize

that it's locked. I decide to try to kick the door in. I take a few steps back and run full speed to the door and knock it completely off the hinges. What I saw threw me into a fit of rage. My next door neighbor, someone who I have become extremely close with, was in my bed, with my boyfriend, and her best friend too! I growled, charged at them and started snatching weaves and hoes everywhere.

I had the one who I thought was my friend, Lena, hemmed up against the wall and her best friend whose name I don't even care to remember, comes behind me and tries to get a sucker punch in but, Cane grabs her and tosses her like a rag doll out of the room. Next, I'm dragging Lena's slut bucket ass out of my house. When I make it back to

the room, Cane has some clothes on and is talking about, "Let me explain." I don't want to hear it. I had just come home from aborting our child and here he was having a fucking threesome in our house, in our bed. I was so overwhelmed with emotions that I just collapsed right there in the middle of the floor. He instantly ran to me because he must have thought that I fainted. I just couldn't take this anymore. In between my sobs, I told him to get his stuff and leave the house because I just couldn't look at him at that moment.

He wouldn't leave me in that state though. I didn't even have the strength to fight him so I just lay there on the floor in the fetal position crying my poor heart out. He gets up and goes somewhere and I was hoping

that he was leaving but then, he comes and picks me up and takes me to the bathroom where there is water running in the bathtub for me. He begins to strip me of my clothes and puts me in the warm water and proceeds to bathe me. We don't say anything. What is there to say? When he is done bathing me, he stands me up, dries me off, and pulls one of his t-shirts over my head. He picks me up again and takes me to the bedroom and gently places me in our bed. I don't know when he changed the sheets and I don't care because as soon as my head hits the pillow, I am out like a light.

CHAPTER 8

I am awake and don't know what time it is
but I do know that it is dark out and every
light is off in the house. I didn't mind
though. I guess it was the state of mind that
I was in. I needed to get up though because
I really needed to relieve my bladder. I get
out of the bed and head to the bathroom
only to run into something solid at the door.
I know that it wasn't the door because I
remembered knocking it off the hinges.
Suddenly, I forgot about my bladder. A hand
quickly goes around my neck and begins to
choke me. The person pushes me with force
back to the bed and throws me on it. I try to
scramble away but, this person grabs me by
my ankles and pulls me back. It's safe to say

that it's a guy and I am absolutely positive that I know what he wants. He keeps me bound with my hands above my head and I hear something metal clink together. He handcuffs my hands together. I am so afraid that I forget to scream in fear of what more he may do to me. "What do you want and who are you?" I ask him. He pauses with his movements but does not answer and continues to push me up to the head board. He undoes one handcuff and wraps it around one of the bars so that I can't move.

I am so mentally and physically tired that I still can't scream but the tears are pouring out of my eyes like a river. He finally speaks. "I've been watching you." A chill runs down my spine. "I know that your kids aren't here and your man ain't neither. I saw when he

brought those girls into y'all house. He chuckles. "That dude is stupid. I also know about your past and you having to do whatever you had to just to support your kids because he wasn't really helping you. I know everything. I've wanted you for some time now and I've just been waiting for the right moment to take you." I tense up even more. With a trembling voice I ask, "Take me where?" He chuckles again. "You know what I mean, baby. Now hold still and don't fight this." He begins to tear my shirt open and I remember that Cane didn't put any underwear on me. He notices that and I can feel a sinister smile come across his face. A pair of headlights appears across the dark room and I see a masked man above me. He has on a fitted black shirt and the mask is

black. His eyes; they stare back at me and it was something in them that made me pause. The front door knob jiggles and I hear Cane trying to get in but the chain is on the door.

Curious, I ask this masked man, "How did you get in here?" He chuckles again. "I have my ways" He undoes the handcuffs and tells me that we will meet again and then he disappears into the house somewhere. I am frozen in place for fear that he will change his mind and try to take me with him. The beating on the door gets louder and I snap out of it and I go to unlock the door and let Cane in. As soon as he walks in he asks, "Why'd you have the chain on the door?" I replied, "You left me in this house by myself, Cane. What did you expect?" He

looked at me like he wanted to say something else but, I just walked off. He tried to follow me in the room but I stopped him. "Where do you think you're going?" I say. "To get in bed" he says. "No you're sleeping on the couch. You know where the extra blankets are. He sucks his teeth and I snap my head to the side. He knew better than to challenge me at this moment. "Yo! Why is my shirt ripped like that?" He says looking at me funny. "I didn't want your stank ass shirt on me and when I was about to rip it off, your ass came to the door." I then turn around and walk into the room. Thank God that he didn't follow me. I got back into bed and lay down. After the night I had, I couldn't sleep. I stay awake the rest of the night thinking about the masked

man. I don't know why I didn't tell Cane

what happened.

CHAPTER 9

It's been several years and our kids are now old enough to understand the things that Cane and I are going through. Call me crazy for still being with him but, we want our kids to grow up in a two parent home. We didn't have that growing up and a parent only wants what's best for their kids. To date, Cane and I have never fought in front of our kids and we don't plan to. They are both so smart. Kel, who's seven now and Kim, who's five, excel in school at such young ages and we're so very proud of them. Even though we put on an act for our kids, our relationship is in disarray. We both have someone else on the side. We both know of each other's unfaithfulness and

even still, we co-exist for the sake of the kids.

The kids still spend a lot of time with my mom and now with his parents as well, so we don't have to pretend much. Cane is never home and I don't mind at all because I spend all my extra time with DJ. He is the dude that I've been seeing. We kind of just ran into each other at the Supermarket. I was rushing to make it home and cook because we had family coming over for the Fourth of July. I was rushing down the aisle not really paying any attention and texting on my phone and I ran right into him. It felt like a brick wall. I looked up and he was smiling down at me. I am very short, 5'3, to be exact. He looked to be about at least 6 ft

tall. After the apologies, we exchanged numbers and the rest is history.

He does the things for me that Cane does not do. He wines and dines me, sends me flowers just because, and whispers sweet nothings in my ear. In the back of my mind I think that he is too good to be true because of the guys that I've dealt with and the life that I've lived but, I try to ignore it. There's something about him though and I just can't put my finger on it.

One day Cane comes home and doesn't say a word to me. He just starts packing his bags. He's taking clothes out of his closet straight off the hangers and taking them to his car. He is throwing his socks and underwear into plastic grocery bags and his

other clothes are going in garbage bags. I finally ask him where he's going. "I'm leaving you! I'm going to stay with Gina. She is the "other woman". He met her when he started working at this warehouse about a year ago. "How are your kids and I supposed to live off of my income? You know that I can't afford this rent." I begin to panic because my job does not pay enough for me to handle rent and utilities and I don't want to live with anybody else. I would hate to revert back to my old ways of getting money, and I definitely will not ask DJ for anything. "I'll help you pay rent this month but, you have to figure something else out" he says. "What happened to you never hurting me and never leaving me?

Huh?" I began to cry because I was caught completely by surprise.

"Look! We both haven't been happy for a long time and I am tired of all the fussing and fighting. I still want to see my kids but, we need to be a part." With that, he walked out of my life. I know that we both had someone else but, I had given this man over eight years of my life. It wasn't that easy to let go. But they say, "In order to get over one man, get up under another one"and that's exactly what I was about to do. I just couldn't shake the depressed state that I was in. With Cane leaving, it affected me more than I wanted to admit but, I will bounce back because I had DJ to soften the blow.

DJ's real name is David Jackson. I nicknamed him DJ because David just doesn't fit him. I called him up after Cane left and he came right over. Remember that I told y'all that it was something strange about him? Well, that feeling hasn't gone away. It just keeps nagging at me. I really don't know why though because he hasn't given me any signs that put up a red flag besides him being the perfect gentleman.

He comes over later that night and we are just talking and watching television when all of a sudden, he grabs me up off of the couch and throws me on the floor. Of course I am alarmed because he was always so gentle. He has never raised his voice or anything before today and I am so shocked right now. "Do you know how long I've

waited to get you alone and to myself?" he asks me. I have never been alone with DJ because of that feeling I've had about him. I was always out in public or around certain family members when I would meet up with him. "By the way that you just threw me down, I can imagine" I say trying to keep my voice from calm. I put a smirk on my face to hide the fact that I am afraid of what he may do. I mean I like the kinky shit but, he was a little too rough. "What's up?" I ask. He gets on top of me on the floor and I pretty much know where his mind is at now. DJ and I have never had sex before and not because I didn't want to. I was trying to wait for a change, give him something to look forward to. "Do you think that we are ready? You don't think that it's

too soon?" I ask. "Hell yeah, we ready" he says in a high pitched voice. I promise that I'll be gentle. He knows that it has been a while for me and I am in a vulnerable state. I shouldn't be doing this now. I need this though. To feel wanted meant a lot to me because Cane has made me feel like an obligation for so long. I just wanted to feel loved. Finally giving in to him, DJ put it on me. He had me speaking tongues. He even had tears coming from my eyes. But, the saying goes, one night of pleasure will cause you a lifetime of pain.

The weeks following our first time and only time, DJ made my life a living hell! When he wasn't calling my phone repeatedly, he was popping up at my house and job unannounced. Everywhere that I went, he

knew where I was. He would send pictures to my phone of me at this and that particular place. No! That's not creepy at all, right?! It had gotten to the point where I had to almost file a report on him. I mean, I know that my cookie was good and all that but, I didn't know that it would make the boys go crazy.

I called him before I filed a restraining order on him to see where his head was and to get him to stop. <Ring, Ring> He picks up and I don't give him the chance to speak. "DJ, it's been fun. Well, it was fun until you changed up on me and got psycho but, we have to go our separate ways now." There was a long pause. "Hello? Are you still there?" I had to ask. "I love you, Kimme!" He throws this bombshell on me and I

almost want to continue our relationship. ALMOST! "You don't love me. We've only been fooling around for about eight months. Look! I can't do this. It's over!" I say getting frustrated and tired of this conversation. "I do love you, Kimme. I've loved you for a long time." His voice changed. It had gotten deeper if that was possible. It kind of reminded me of…. No! It couldn't be. My mind was playing tricks on me. "I told you that we would see each other again didn't I, Kimme?"

Just then, it all made sense to me. The uneasy feeling that I've always had about him was just my instincts. His body and his movements were so familiar now. Those eyes are the same eyes of the man who came into my house years ago. How did I

not pay closer attention? "Now that I have you to myself, I am never letting you go. If I can't have you, no one will." The hell! This fool is crazy for real. I end the call and soon after, my phone rings. I jump at the sound because now, I'm paranoid. I check the ID on my cell and see that it's Cane. I roll my eyes, breathe a sigh of relief and then answer.

CHAPTER 10

"Hello! How are you doing? Did you miss me? I pull the phone away from my ear and roll my eyes because I haven't heard from this dude in about three weeks and he calls me with this mess. He has been keeping in touch with his kids through my mom since that's where they are most of the time. "Why should I miss something that I never really had?" I said sarcastically. He chuckles then says, "Girl, you know that this is your dick stop tripping." "Well, last time I checked, that dick belongs to Gina now" I threw back at him. Before he could reply there was this loud boom at my door. I tell Cane to hold on but continue to hold the phone to my ear. As I'm walking to the door

there is another loud boom and I jump in fear. Cane asks me who it is and I don't know but, I have an idea. I am afraid to ask but I find the courage to. "Who's there?" My voice does not sound like my own and it shouldn't because a crazy person is trying to break my door down.

"Open the door, Bitch! You think that you can just leave me alone, just toss me to the side when you're done with me? We're not done until I say that we're done. Now open this door before I tear this motherfucker down!" This ninja is ill! I had a feeling that DJ didn't have all of his marbles and I was right. He is missing a few screws. I snap out of my thoughts when I realize that Cane is yelling through the phone asking me who's that and what does he want. "He's just

some guy that I was messing around with but cut him off because he was getting too crazy. **<Boom! Boom! Boom! Crack!>** The door comes crashing down and I back up so that the door does not hit me and it hits the floor with a loud thud. I scream and try to run and slip on my phone that I hadn't realized that I'd dropped.

DJ grabs me by my ankles and pulls me toward him. "Come back here! You can't get away from me. I love you until death. I will kill you for trying to leave me". I am crying and fighting trying to get away from this man but he has a vice grip on me and his hands are snaking their way to my neck. "If you scream again, I'll break your fucking neck. Now, get up!" He drags me to my

room and when he sees my unmade bed, he just snaps again. "Who the fuck have you had in our bed?" Our bed! When did he move in? He picks me up, slaps me and throws me on the bed. "Please stop, DJ. I'm sorry for trying to leave you but, you scared me and I didn't know what else to do." I tried to reason with him and it seemed to be working because the coldness in his eyes softened a little. "I never wanted to hurt you, Kimma. Ever since I saw you I've wanted you. When I came into your apartment that night years ago, I was ready to shower you with my love but, your punk ass baby daddy came back home and ruined it for us. Let's run away together and leave everything behind; just me and you." He has this crazed look in his eyes. "What

about my kids and my family?" I say not being able to stop the tears from falling from my eyes. "Forget about them. We can have our own kids and then we can be your family." Now I know that this dude has lost his mind to think that I'd leave my kids and family behind.

I was wondering why no one had called the police especially since I know how nosey my neighbors are. As my mind begins to wonder, I see a shadow out of the corner of my eye and before I know it there is a loud pop and DJ's grip loosens on me and he falls to the floor in pain. I look up to find Cane standing over my bed and then, everything turns black.

I awaken to find myself in my bed wrapped in some covers. I hear a noise and immediately begin to panic. I search around my room with my eyes because I don't want to move too much in the bed and draw attention to myself just in case DJ is still here. I spot one of my heels on the floor by my closet door. Whoever is in my house starts to make their way back to my bedroom. So, I leap out of the bed and grab the shoe just in time to see Cane standing at my door looking confused as to what I was doing. Once I realized it was him I began to get light headed and swoon like I was about to pass out. He put the tray down that was in his hands and ran over to me.

"Whoa, Baby! You shouldn't be out of bed. The paramedics wanted to take you to the hospital but, since they didn't see or detect anything major wrong with you; they said that you could stay home and get some rest. I just decided to stay here and take care of you" he explained. It didn't feel like anything was wrong besides me feeling light-headed. So, I didn't argue about that. "Where's DJ? Did you kill him?" I fire questions back to back at him. By this time he has placed me back in the bed and is seated next to me. "Hold on, girl! One question at a time. I shot him in the back and he didn't die. He is at the hospital being treated and once he's released, he will be arrested for his assault on you. The detectives came by while you were still

unconscious. I told them what I know, which wasn't much. Once you feel better, they need for you to come to the station and give your statement. I had an uneasy feeling about DJ still being alive but, right now there was nothing that could be done.

He blew out a breath. "I heard when he broke the door down and I heard a lot of tussling in the background. I rushed over as fast as I could." I just nodded my head. I could tell that Cane wanted to say more. I prepared myself. "Who was dude and where did you meet this clown?" I knew it was coming. I took a deep breath. "I met him at the store. That time we had family coming for The Fourth of July. Remember that?" He nods so I continue. "He seemed nice so I continued to communicate with

him. I knew that it was something about him. I just couldn't figure it out." There was no way that I was going to tell Cane about when he broke into our house years before. I hadn't told anyone and I planned to take that to my grave. "Well, I'm glad that I came when I did because he probably would've killed you. Has he ever been around our kids?" He looked like he was going to slap me if I said yes. So, I said no. It was the truth though but, why did I feel so guilty. I felt like I brought all of this on myself. I was exhausted from the events of the day. So, I told Cane that I needed a nap. "Did they fix the door?" I don't know who "they" were but knowing Cane, it was already done. "Yeah! I got you, Baby. I am going to stay the night with you so you won't have to

worry about anything. If you're hungry, I made you some sandwiches. There's chips and juice right there". He pointed at the tray that he was carrying earlier. "Nah! I'm good; just tired" I yawn. He nodded and began to make his way over to what used to be his side of the bed. I stop him though because he is no longer mine. "Uh! You can stay but, you will be sleeping on the couch. You have Gina now and you can't be dipping back and forth". He sighs but goes in the hall closet and gets a blanket. He says goodnight and turns off all the lights. I call his name and he comes back in the room, "Thank you, Cane! If it wasn't for you showing up when you did, you would probably be helping my parents plan my

funeral." He just nods and heads to the couch.

I lay down but, can't fall asleep and with the night that I've had, could you blame me? Men! I don't think that I'll ever be able to figure them out. Men say that women are complicated. Tuh!

CHAPTER 11

The next day, after going down to the police station, I went to check on my kids. Sometimes I think that my mom thinks that they are her kids because she never wants them to come home. My sisters and I are all grown and doing our own thing now. Even though I am the only one with kids and living on my own, my sisters are never there. So, I think that she gets lonely in this big house by herself.

I didn't tell my mom about the incident with DJ because I didn't want to worry her and didn't feel like playing 21 questions. Besides, it is over now. My kids were happy to see me but as soon as I asked were they ready to come home, they ran back to their

grandma's room. All I could do was shake my head. Kel and Kim were always mistaken for twins and people couldn't believe me when I'd say that they were two years apart. I love my kids and although I was young and was not ready for them, I do not regret them at all. I often think about my baby that I aborted and if we made the right decision. I know that I don't love that baby any less even though he or she isn't here with us. After asking my kids for a third time if they wanted to come home and them rejecting me (sad face...lol), I headed back home.

When I pull up I grab my purse and cock my .45 that Cane got me for my safety. It was dark out and even though they had DJ in custody, I didn't want to risk it. I get into

the house safely but, I go through the house turning on all of the lights and checking every room. Everything looked to be normal so I breathed a sigh of relief just as someone knocked on the door. I cocked the gun again and asked who it was. "Cane!" he said. He still had his key. Yet, I appreciated him for at least respecting me to knock knowing that he no longer lives here.

I let him in wondering what he was doing here. He had done enough for me and I know that Gina was not pleased with all the time that he had spent here in the last 24 hours. "Hey! I thought that you were going home" I said. He looked at me and took a deep breath. "Gina and I had a fight because she saw my car parked at your house last night." How ironic, huh? He

cheats on me with her, leaves me for her, and comes back to me when they have a fight. "I take it that you didn't let her know that you were coming over here? Did you at least tell her why you were here and what happened?" I ask him. I find this whole thing amusing. "No! She didn't need to know all of that. I was thinking about coming home. I miss coming home to you and the kids". He paused. I guess he was expecting me to say something. I just couldn't believe him. I feel like if I wasn't good enough before he left me, what makes me good enough now? Or, did he just find out that the grass isn't greener on the other side?!

 Either way, I wasn't ready to let him back into my house yet. I guess he had other

plans though. "I'm coming back home! That way, I can help you pay the rent and I want to get married". He had to be kidding right? This dude was crazy if he thought that I would just up and marry him after he left me for another broad. "Hold on! How are you gone come in here demanding stuff? I may not be ready for you to come back so soon. If you really want to help me, you'd pay the rent anyway knowing that your kids live here. As for us getting married, No! I can't trust that you'd do right by me". He smiles at me and goes to his car to get his clothes that I found out he never removed from the trunk of his car. I didn't argue much because I did miss him. I let him come back because he was right. Our kids needed us together and we wanted them to have a

life that we never had. But as usual, Cane was going to be Cane and it didn't take long before I found out that he was messing with one of our neighbors.

CHAPTER 12

<Boom, Boom, Boom>

"Open up this door because I know he's in there" I yell, beating on the trick's door where I know Cane has his no good ass at. The chick's brother opens the door and I storm past him and go straight to her room. She lives in the apartment underneath us and I had been in her apartment before so I know exactly where her room is. I beat on her bedroom door and her brother was tussling with my cousin, Phil, who I brought along with me in case some stuff jumped off.

I heard some moving around behind the door and I thought I heard Cane's voice. So, I took a few steps back and ran and bust the

door down. I caught her still in the bed with covers pulled up to her chin and Cane's ass jumping out of her window. I ran to her and gave her a three piece because she knew he was my man and she used to break her neck speaking to me knowing that she was fooling around with him behind my back.

I didn't even give her a chance to fight back before I ran out to catch up with Cane. By the time I made it outside, Cane was nowhere in sight. I called his phone but he kept sending it to voicemail. I then called his mom and left a nice little message for him because I knew that is where he was headed. His mom was a cool lady and we often had talks about Cane and his father and how she went through the same thing with him even though they had been

married for over 30 years. Cane's father wasn't there for him because he was always working and in the streets. Like father, like son. His mom is always trying to get us to talk out our problems and be there for our kids but I am getting tired of the back and forth with this man.

She immediately calls me back and I fill her in on our latest drama and we get off of the phone. I didn't feel like much talking. I was just ready to go upside this dude head. I didn't know that I wouldn't see him until a week later.

I am laying in bed about to doze off. My kids have finally decided to come home and spend time with mommy. We have been busy all day at the park, shopping, and we

went out to eat. I don't know what my mom is doing to my kids but they love it over there so much that I just have to love on them when they are home. I hear keys jingle in the door. I know no one else has keys to my house and I automatically know that it's Cane. I should have changed the locks. He walks in and puts his keys on the table and I hear a light come on. I look up and see that he is in the kid's doorway to their room watching them sleep. He smiles then goes in to kiss them I assume. He turns the light out and heads to our room. I close my eyes and play possum. He doesn't turn on the light. He sits on the bed. "Kimme, are you asleep?" I ignore his ass. He takes a deep breath and takes his shoes off and then lies down. "I know that you aren't

asleep and I'm sorry. You have been giving me a hard time since I came back and we weren't having sex. A man has needs and I was tired of begging you. I shouldn't have to beg my woman to sleep with me and you never gave me an answer on us getting married. I was angry".

I just laid there because right now I didn't have the energy to argue with him and I didn't want to know where he'd been this past week. I simply said, "You do you and I'll do me. That's what you want, right? I don't really think you know what you want. I'm good! Two can play this game". I didn't want to get back in these streets but something had to give. "Be careful what you ask for Kimme because you know when I really get out there, ain't no stopping me!" I

laughed in his face. "Dude, you been out there. It's just now you don't have to hide it. Just respect our parents and kids and we straight. Just don't bring that mess to our house."

With that, I turned my back on him and was headed back to sleep when my phone vibrated letting me know that I had a text message. I opened it up and smiled because it was just the person that I needed to hear from.

CHAPTER 13

I was at this hotel meeting up with this dude and it felt weird. It felt like I was having an out of body experience. It has been a while since I've "stepped out" on Cane and I must admit that I was having second thoughts. One, it was too many diseases out there; two, I was just used to one man now. After Cane gave me my first "gift" though at least I was smart and started wrapping it up.

I knock on the door after I finally get up the nerves to get out of the car. After the second knock, he opens the door and I am overpowered by blunt smoke. "I've been waiting on you, Kimme. What took you so long?" he says while looking me up and

down like I am a piece of meat. Now, I am not a skinny woman, never have been. I have a decent shape and when I feel like looking pretty, I can turn some heads. I take a deep breath and walk into the room. I can tell that he was getting himself prepared for my arrival because I saw a bottle of liquor on the table and I could see that this wasn't the first blunt that he had smoked. I took a seat at the table and I heard the door click behind me. He came up behind me and began to massage my shoulders. I guess he noticed how tense I was.

"Ain't no need to be uptight. We both know why we're here. I'll try to make this as comfortable as possible for you" he breathed in my ear and it sent shivers down my spine. I couldn't believe that he still has

this affect on me after all of these years. He was my first and they say that you never get over your first. My, oh my, how I've tried because he is no good for me. Us being here tonight still somehow felt odd. "I see that the cat has your tongue but we don't have to talk" he says. He grabs my hands and leads me to the bed. He pushes me gently down and takes off all of my clothes. I don't say anything for fear of me telling him to stop and I didn't want him to. I needed this stress reliever for all of the crap that I've been through with Cane and life period. It's true that I am to blame for most of the things possibly and it's true that this man that I am here with now has inflicted some of that pain on me as well but, I knew that he would satisfy my craving.

Again I say; one night of passion could lead to a lifetime of pain and bringing Mercy back into my life could possibly be one of the biggest mistakes of my life.

CHAPTER 14

"What's up? I need you to meet me at the spot". I am sitting looking at my phone and trying to figure out a lie that I can tell to get out of the house. Mercy and I have been doing our thing again for about a year. I've heard that Cane has been busy but I haven't caught him and if he's seen or heard anything about me, he hasn't mentioned it. We agreed that we would do our own thing, so why was I sneaking?

We were in a new and bigger place now. Our kids were home all of the time now and I guess they've just gotten older and want to be in their own rooms. Whatever the reason, I was happy that they have been staying with me. Cane and I were back to

putting on a show. Some days and some things were genuine. The rest was just for show though. We'd have sex occasionally and that was it. I get another text and its Mercy asking if I was still coming. I go upstairs and tell Cane that I'm going to my Mom's house. He's on his phone probably planning the same thing that I am. He says, okay and I am out the door.

I meet Mercy at what has become our regular hotel room that we rent every time that he comes home. Having an uneasy feeling about being with him has diminished and I just go with the flow. I do things with Mercy that I don't do with Cane. I even once considered a threesome with him and one of his homeboys. I came to my senses at the last minute because I may be a freak

but, I want to reserve something for my husband; whoever that may be.

When I made it to the room, Mercy had the door cracked open. I just walked right in. He was lying on the bed in his birthday suit and standing at attention. I chuckled and shut the door. I am sure that he wouldn't mind if someone caught a glimpse of his manhood. God had blessed him in that area and he knew how to use it. "Look who's anxious!" I say as I begin to take my clothes off. I begin to walk towards the bed and as I begin to get in, he tells me to get in on all fours. I don't question him because we were always doing kinky things.

I get in on my knees and he stands up in the bed. Me and his manhood are having a

faceoff. I look up to him and he's smirking down at me. "Whatchu waitin on? Handle your business" he says. I don't need any more persuading and I get to work. I must have been doing a good job because he almost fell a couple of times. I assume that he was about to cum because he took himself out of my mouth and it makes a popping sound because I was still putting in work. He flips me over and begins to rub my body up and down. He lay atop of me and I could feel his breath on my ear. I am extremely turned on and I am literally trembling just from his touch.

Why does this man still have this affect on me? He has hurt me so bad and is the cause of my wild lifestyle. Yet, I continue to come back for more. I just can't break free from

him and if I believed in black magic, I'd be sure that he had a hex on me. "Tonight, I am going to take you from the back, back" he says. For those of you who don't know, that's anal. I've tried it before with Cane but, Mercy has never done it and we've had this conversation about me letting him try it on me. Always doing whatever he asked, I agreed to it. Like I said we've tried pretty much everything. If I didn't know any better, I'd think we were together again or married instead of Cane and I.

I shudder when he licks my ear. "What's wrong?" he asked. I was afraid to speak for fear that nothing would come out. So, I just shook my head. He chuckled. I think it turned him on or made him feel powerful with how weak he made me. Cane used to

make me feel this way but, he didn't have this affect on me anymore. Mercy reached over me and got something off of the bed side table. He sat up in the bed and then rubbed something cold between my butt cheeks. I assumed that it was lubricant. He asked me if I was ready and went in. I reached behind me and gripped his thighs to hold him at a steady pace because although I've done this before, it's been awhile. Soon we got our rhythm and it was pure bliss from there. He turned me in all kinds of positions. Once he was hitting it so hard, we fell out of the bed. We were in our zone. Before you know it, we were both out like a light from all of the sex that we'd had.

I am awakened by the sound of a ringing phone. I rolled over and was about to go

back to sleep when I realized that it was my phone ringing. I looked at the clock and shot straight up because it was almost 2am. I rushed and put my clothes on careful not to wake Mercy up. I grabbed my phone and my keys and left the hotel. I shot him a text to let him know that I would talk to him later and just headed over to my Mom's house. My phone rang again and it was Cane. I didn't answer. I had my story straight for when I did see him later today.

As I was pulling up to my Mom's house, I saw Cane's '97 Cutlass sitting outside and he was standing next to it holding his phone. I knew it was about to be trouble so I jumped out of my car and started questioning him before he could even speak. "Where have you been? I've been

riding around looking for you for hours" I shouted. "Who have you been with because you haven't been at home, your Mom's, or your sister's house? So, don't lie". I was being so dramatic and it was probably because my adrenaline was so high and I knew what I had been doing all night.

He looked at me and shook his head. "Girl, gone on with all that. I ain't asking you where you been because we both know that you weren't looking for me. Don't worry about where I been. I need to get in the house to change clothes because I lost my key." he says. "Where you about to go?" I ask him with my nose turned up. "Don't worry about that. Ain't you staying with your mom tonight or whatever?" I just paused. So, he continued. "I am about to go

out with my homeboys. I might be back about five" he said and was getting in his car. I knew that he was still fooling around with Gina because I went through his phone a few weeks back. Don't ask me why because I don't know. I guess that I still care but, he won't know how hurt I am behind finding out. "I'm out" he says. "Go do what you were doing before you came back to your Mom's house". He peeled off. I can't stand that bastard. I swear if it wasn't for our kids, I'd been gone.

I looked at my phone and saw a text message from Mercy. ***Come back.*** I jumped back in my car and headed back to the hotel to give Mercy some more. Hell! I couldn't let Cane have all of the fun! I was

so tired of these no good men doing me any kind of way. Yea! I'm a pushover but, come on now. I deserve to be happy just like anybody else.

CHAPTER 15

Cane was out with one of his groupies as usual and Mercy was gone back home. I didn't have him on my mind though because before he left, he told me that I could only be his side piece. I would never be his girlfriend again. It hurt me so bad but, forget him. At this point in my life I was lonely and miserable.

One day, I called up my sister Quanna. She was dating this guy named Ethan and he had this friend named Trent that had been trying to holla at me for a while now. So, I said what the hell. I may as well give him a try. I've got nothing to lose anyway when it comes to men. I was still with Cane if you wanted to call it that. We could see each

other out with someone else and we'd pass right by each other like we didn't know one another. It was never spoken of when we would make it home at night if we made it there at all.

After a while though, Trent began to get abusive verbally and physically. It all started one night when we were together. He asked me if I loved him. We had talked about it a few times, so it was nothing new. I told him that I was falling for him. I know that it sounded crazy considering that I had a "man" at home but, Cane and I had this "fly by the way" relationship. And to be honest, I was looking for it to end soon. I wanted a way out. Once I told Trent that I was falling for him though, things changed.

We were together the following night after I revealed that to him and we were just cuddling up watching TV at his house. He told me to go and fix him something to drink and I told him that I was tired and didn't feel like getting up. All of a sudden, he slapped me. He then asked me if I loved him. I said, yes. He slapped me again. I was dazed and confused at first because this came from out of nowhere. Then, he slapped me again. I was about to say something but, then he punched me in the mouth. I am scared and I am now trying to figure out how to get out of there. "This pussy belongs to me. Do you understand?" he shouted. I didn't say anything because my mouth is now bleeding everywhere.

My silence earned me another punch to the face. "Trent, why are you doing this? I thought that you loved me?" I cried. "I don't love you bitch! I just wanted you to fall in love with me so that I could use and treat you the way that I wanted. You were easier than I thought though. I should have known better because your own baby daddy doesn't even want you. I see him all over town parading his hoes around and, you're so stupid because you stay with him. I don't want no dumb broad. Besides, you're too fat for me anyways. Having sex with you and getting any and everything out of you that I can is all that you're good for.

By this time, I am crying so hard that I could barely breathe and it's possible that it could be because he had his knee in my

chest. He snatches me up by my hair and drags me to his bedroom. All the while, I am kicking and screaming. He stops a couple of times to yell for me to shut up and continuously kicks me. He pulls me up and begins to choke me. "Shut up! If you scream one more time, I'll kill you and then go and kill your kids and baby daddy". The look in his eyes said that he was serious. How did I miss this again? I thought that I was being cautious. Yet, here I am fighting for my life again.

Trent slapped me because he was talking to me and I didn't answer him fast enough. I realized then that he had some rope in his hands and I thought the worst. Tears started to fall down my face even more. He reached behind him and pulled out a gun.

"Make one more sound and this shit is over" he whispered in my ear. I closed my eyes as more tears fell and all I could think about were my kids and how much more time that I could've spent with them and their smiling faces.

I willed myself to open my eyes and he had the gun in the middle of my forehead. This bastard had the nerves to have a smirk on his face. "Get in the bed" he demanded of me in an eerily calm voice. I did what I was told and he put the gun down. He proceeded to tie me up to the headboard and my feet to the end posts of the bed. I am lying there spread eagle wondering what he was going to do with me. He climbed onto the bed and began to rip my clothes off of me with a box cutter that he

got out of a drawer. When I was down to my underwear, he saw that my cycle was on and I was relieved because I knew that most men wouldn't want anything to do with a woman in that state. My relief was short lived thought because he pulled my underwear and pad off like he didn't even see it. He began to take his clothes off too and I began to cry and beg for him not to do this.

"Shut up! You ought to be glad somebody wants some of your pussy with your fat ass. I wasn't fat. Sure I had some more extra weight than the average; this dude has some serious issues. He got on the bed and crawled up to me and forced himself inside of me as hard as he could, all the while calling me out of my name. "For you to be

fat, you sure do have some good pussy".
After that, he came inside of me and got up
off the bed and went to the bathroom.
Thank God that I was on birth control
because I would go insane if I were to have
a baby by this man. I heard the shower start
and burst out into a fit of crying.

 After leaving me there for a few days with
no shower or being able to go to the
restroom, I lie still tied to this bed in my
own urine and feces while he continuously
raped and abused me. Then, he came in
one day and cut the ropes and told me that
I could go. Just like that! He told me that if I
told anyone, he would kill my entire family.
With that, he left me alone and told me to
lock his door when I left. I'm looking like
"what the fuck?" I pulled on one of his

oversized t-shirts and jogging pants and got the hell out of there. I made it home and took the longest shower and passed out.

I awaken to the ringing of my phone. I thought that it was the next day but it was just 8:47pm when I looked at the clock. I pick up my ringing phone wondering why the person hasn't hung up yet. The number is unfamiliar to me but I answer it anyway. When I picked up, all I heard was heavy breathing and then, they hung up. I don't have the energy to try and figure this mess out. I checked my phone and saw that I had several missed calls. I check my messages and call my mom to check on my kids. She is a God send. My kids live with me now but they go to school from her house since she lives in the school district. My mom answers

the phone, "Where have you been and why haven't you been answering your phone? Is everything all right?" she asked with worry etched in her voice. "Ma, I'm fine. I haven't been feeling well that's all" I told her.

Why didn't I tell her what happened? Why couldn't I expose Trent? Why didn't I go to the police? You didn't see the look in his eyes when he told me not to. I was scared and didn't want anything to happen to my family. He stalked me and kept tabs on me daily until one day, I didn't see him anymore. It was like he fell off the face of the earth.

CHAPTER 16

For the next couple of months I wasn't myself. I wouldn't talk unless spoken to and my personality was nonexistent. And let's not talk about my self esteem. I still hadn't heard from Trent and I was relieved. I didn't give a damn if I never saw that sick son of bitch ever again. I still hadn't told anyone what he'd done to me and I'm sure that was what was tearing me up inside. I hadn't heard from Cane. My mom says he's been keeping in touch with the kids and spending time with them at least.

Mercy has been trying to get in contact with me only to have sex. I haven't responded to him. I haven't had the energy

or desire for it since the Trent incident. I am not myself anymore.

 Knock, Knock, Knock I hear someone knock on my door but I ignore it. Someone has been coming by everyday for the past two weeks knocking and beating on my door. I've shut the entire world out. I haven't been to work in a month and haven't left my apartment in three weeks. I am sure that I no longer have a job because they stopped calling me two weeks ago. I haven't eaten much so I know that I've lost weight but, I was afraid to look at my reflection. I just sit at home in the dark all day. No tv, no nothing. My mom is the only person who knows that I am alive. Hell! She's the reason that my phone is still on. I talk to her and my kids and that's it. Today,

whoever is knocking is persistent though. I continue to ignore them and go get in the shower. They'll eventually go away. At least that's what I was hoping.

While in the shower, I begin to reflect on my life. I am pathetic, I know. I am a few years from being 30 and I haven't accomplished anything. I am always working these dead end jobs. I can't find a good and respectable man and my kids never want to be at home. I know that they love me but, you see, my mind was gone and it was playing tricks on me. I began to cry and I slid down to the floor of the shower. I start to think that this life isn't for me. I absentmindedly get out of the shower and go to my kitchen and get a knife out of the drawer. I am soaking wet and cold but it

doesn't register in my head. I get back in the shower where I've left the water running. I sit back on the floor of the shower and close my eyes. The last thing that I remember is me praying that my mom and kids could forgive me. I pass out losing too much blood from the cut on my wrist I'd just given myself.

I heard knocking again and I know that it wasn't possible if I'm supposed to be dead. Then, I heard a loud boom, running water, and what sounded like something crashing. I felt really tired and I could barely keep my eyes open. I heard my name and then my eyes closed again. Finally! Peace! I hear someone say, "Stay with me". Then, there was peace again. I hear someone say,

"Kimme, come back"! Then, there was peace again.

I open my eyes to bright lights. I closed them so that they could adjust. When I open them again, I quickly realize that I am in a hospital room. The beeping machines gave it away. I looked around the room but it was empty. Just then, the door to the room opens and in walks no one other than Cane himself.

Why is he here and why am I not dead is all that I could think of. Or maybe, I'm in hell and I just can't get away from this dude. He was looking down at his phone when he walked in but he looked up and saw my eyes open and his phone slipped out of his hands. We just stared at each

other for a while. I don't know what he was thinking but, he looks like he hasn't slept in days. He walked out of the room and when he came back in, a woman in a white coat followed. Her name tag said Dr. Bell. She asked if I knew where I was and I shook my head, yes. She proceeded to ask me if I knew who Cane was and I shook my head yes again. I didn't want to talk and I was afraid that I couldn't. I remained quiet. She checked my vital signs, explained to me my treatment and the medicine that I'd be taking and then, she left me alone.

 Over the course of the next couple of days, several people came to my room: my mom and kids, the police to get a statement from me, the doctor, and a host of nurses. Of course, Cane stayed by my side. Why? I

don't know. They even sent in a phyciatrist. I just would not talk. I was happy to see my mom and kids and my sisters even came by a few times. They suggested that I go to a mental institution but my mother and Cane weren't having it. So, they agreed to come by my house twice a week to "consult" with me.

Once I was released from the hospital and back home, Cane kind of moved back in. My mom wanted me to come home with her but Cane assured her that he'd take care of me. He took a leave from work and my mom would check on me every day, cook and bring food over, and she kept the kids for us. My wrist was still bandaged up and Cane changed and cleaned it twice a day. I still wasn't talking to anyone though. Cane

had to bathe me and feed me or at least attempt to because I wouldn't even eat or do anything for myself.

One day while he was changing my bandage he looked at me and said, "What happened to you, Ma?" He looked at me for an answer and when he didn't get one he said, "Look at me, Kimme!" When I looked at him I could've sworn that he could see to my soul. I just stared at him and eventually he just sighed and left me alone. I didn't have any words to say. I wanted my life to be over and I am still not quite sure who saved me but they should have left me to my fate.

I looked out of the window that Cane had left open to let some fresh air in and all of a

sudden a breeze came in and blew across my face. I closed my eyes and for the first time in my life, I felt that everything would be all right. But, how do I begin to put the pieces of my life back together?

CHAPTER 17

It had been a month and a half since my second failed attempt at suicide and I still didn't know who got me to the hospital in time. The doctor said had I lost anymore blood I would've surely died. Cane was still there and I had to wonder why. Before this incident, we hadn't talked for months. So, why was he here now? Just then, he walked in my room with a plate of food and I shook my head no. I was afraid to look in the mirror at my reflection because I hadn't eaten much in about six or seven months and, let's not talk about my hair. I am pretty sure that I look like a troll by the head. Cane didn't seem to mind though.

He put the plate down on my night stand as usual in hopes that I'd eat it but I didn't plan to. Before he could make it out of the door I said, "Why are you here?" He stood frozen for a minute before he turned around and looked at me with a shocked expression on his face. My throat burned from not talking for so long but it was manageable. "I thought that you would never talk again. It's good to hear your voice" he said. "Why are you here?" I asked again. He made eye contact with me and then said, "I love you, Kimme! The month before your accident, I had been coming by every other day knocking but you wouldn't answer. The day that I found you, something didn't feel right. I knocked, left, and came back. I heard a loud thump and I panicked thinking that

something was wrong and kicked the door in. I found you in the shower on the floor bleeding and called 911.

I had been coming over to tell you how much I love you and that I want to marry you but, you just wouldn't answer your phone or your door. I knew something was wrong. Tell me what happened" he finally says. I couldn't look at him as the tears began to fall. He hugged me and let me compose myself. It took me a while to compose myself. Once I calmed down, I told him everything. I told him how Trent had been the almost perfect guy and then turned into this crazy monster. I told him how he raped me and held me captive. I even told him about Trent's threat to harm our kids and if I told anyone what he'd done

to me. That really pissed him off. The more I told him, the angrier he got. He let me cry some more and I fell asleep in his arms.

Why was our relationship so complicated? When it was bad, it was really bad but, no matter how bad it was he always seemed to be the one to come to my aid in my time of need. It was like he had a sixth sense for me and my well-being. Did this mean that we were meant to be? All of the cards were stacked against us though. We could never get it right. I just didn't get it.

It had been a week since Cane and I had our talk and I was up and about. I was talking more and the kids were coming back around. Things were beginning to look up. Cane made it home from work and walked

in and gave me a kiss. We weren't officially back together but, I was working on my issues and we were rebuilding our relationship. "Baby, what did you say Trent's last name was?" he asked. "Gray. Why?" I said. "The police found a dude in his car with a gunshot wound to his head on the levee by the water. That's the name that they said was on his identification card. Whoever murdered him didn't take any money or anything though" he continued. I didn't feel any type of way about it but I wondered who served him his dose of karma. I didn't dwell on it for too long. Life goes on, I guess.

EPILOGUE

Have you ever felt like God had just given up on you and that He was playing this game with your life? Well, I felt like that at this very moment. It has been a little over a year since I've learned of Trent's demise and even though I got over that hell, I find myself in a whole other hell. The person delivering this new dish is my husband.

I married Cane! Over the past year and a half, we've had another child, a little girl, Jamie. She looks just like him. She's three months and so precious. I am surprised that she's so timid because Cane stressed me out throughout my entire pregnancy with her. I am shocked that she doesn't cry as often as I did. My kids have been the only

happiness that I've seen in a while and, I know what you may be thinking. Why did I marry him after all of the crap that he had put me through? I believed that he had changed.

Yet, here I am currently sitting at home bouncing our baby while he's out with some jump off in our new car. How do I know this? He butt dialed me and I heard them in the car talking about what they were about to do. I instantly recognized the girl's voice because he's been dealing with this one since after we had gotten married. He won't pick up the phone now of course. Typical!

As crazy as it sounds, I still love him. I hear the keys jingle in the door. As soon as I hear the door opening, I jump up and meet him.

"So, you had that tramp in my car, Cane? Why? What the fuck were you thinking?" I fired at him with tears streaming down my face. He was holding me back so that I wouldn't hit him. I was holding Jamie though so I couldn't. I could slap his ass though. Maybe that would knock some sense into his tail.

"Kay, we haven't had sex since before Jamie was born. I was tired of begging my wife for sex. Resee was available and willing to give me what you wouldn't. You can't blame me for stepping out on you this time because it's your fault. I am left speechless because this man has managed to tear me down again. When I agreed to marry him, I

thought that this part of my life was over. I thought that I would finally be happy.

So, I did the only thing that I could think of. I put Jamie in her crib. I walked to our room closet and reached for my luggage only to move it out of the way. Cane must have thought that I was about to pack some bags to leave him again. He smacked his teeth and turned his back to me because he has seen me pack so many bags and never leave.

I was tired of men treating me like I was scum on the bottom of their shoes. I was not perfect but I was a good woman with a good heart. I am not the same girl that I was a year ago after the "Trent incident". It was

time that I started sticking up for myself and it would start with Cane.

He still had his back to me doing something on his phone until he heard the gun cock. He turned around slowly and his eyes grew wide as he tried to comprehend what was going on. "You know, Cane! I thought that this time was going to be different but, I see that you haven't changed at all. You're still the same hoe ass dude, worse than before. You know of everything that I've been through and yet, you still take me through. I am tired! Any last words?" I ask him as I begin to squeeze the trigger. He couldn't say anything at first. He managed to finally get out, "Wait!" I shook my head. "Time to say, night night,

nigga". I closed my eyes and pulled the trigger *<**BANG! BANG!**>*

"The sweetest woman in the world can be the meanest woman in the world if you make her that way" <It's a thin line between love and hate>

~H-Town~